# Legend of Jungle Land

## The Orphan Girl

SAFIYA WILCOX

Illustrated by Qamer Khatri



This is a work of fiction. All of the characters, names, incidents, organizations, and dialogue in this novel are either the products of the author's imagination or are used fictitiously.

Archway Publishing books may be ordered through booksellers or by contacting:

Archway Publishing
1663 Liberty Drive
Bloomington, IN 47403
www.archwaypublishing.com
844.669.3957

Because of the dynamic nature of the Internet, any web addresses or links contained in this book may have changed since publication and may no longer be valid. The views expressed in this work are solely those of the author and do not necessarily reflect the views of the publisher, and the publisher hereby disclaims any responsibility for them.



ISBN: 978-1-4808-9610-9 (sc)
ISBN: 978-1-4808-9611-6 (e)

Print information available on the last page.

Archway Publishing rev. date: 10/21/2020

Far off in Jungle Land, there was a beautiful castle. In that castle lived a beautiful queen named Autumn. She was the ruler of Jungle Land. She always dreamed of having a daughter of her own. She was loved by all who knew her and those who knew of her. Queen Autumn declared every day to be Happy Day and commanded peace in all the land.

Indeed, there were no problems, and everything was peaceful. Then one day, a little bird named Henta came to the queen. Henta was flapping her wings nervously, darting up and down, and chirping to the queen. She appeared to have a lot to say. Unfortunately, Queen Autumn did not understand what all the chirping was about. Thinking it might be important information, she immediately sent for her interpreters and an artist.

Soon, two interpreters, Kaleb and Adrianna, and one artist, Kaitlyn, presented themselves before the queen. They each listened carefully to the little bird.

Kaleb stood rubbing his chin, nodding, and holding his magnifier over one eye. "Em-hem-em-hem, I see," he said.

Adrianna was careful to get all the details. As she listened, her eyes got bigger and bigger, and she exclaimed, "Shocking! Whatever will we do?"

Once Henta was finished telling them everything, they thanked her and sent her away. They all rushed to the meeting room-except the queen, of course.

After the meeting was done, the queen called a meeting of her own. Queen Autumn had waited so patiently for them, and it was time to find out exactly what was going on in Jungle Land. "What did Henta say?" asked Queen Autumn.

Adrianna replied, "Henta said the land that was once so peaceful now has a raging elephant, stomping and pouncing on the ground and sounding off loud roars throughout the jungle."

"Yes," said Kaleb, "and the other animals are very afraid."

The queen slowly turned away. "That means ... that means," she said.

Everyone else said at the same time, "There is unrest in the animal kingdom!"

"What are we going to do?" asked the queen.

"Don't worry; we will get to the bottom of this," said Kaleb.

They decided to have yet another meeting without the queen. Queen Autumn agreed and dismissed them and trusted them to find a solution. After some thinking, Kaitlyn, Kaleb, and Adrianna had a great idea. Kaitlyn drew the plans on the sketch paper and hung the paper up. They were very proud and certain that it would solve the problem.

The three advisors had whispered and held the magnifying glass to the art as they made plans. They smiled and felt sure that the plan would work. The solution appeared simple enough.

The group sent for the queen. Her heels could be heard clicking and clacking as she came down the long hallway. The large door opened and in walked the queen. Kaitlyn uncovered the picture. It showed a roaring lion chasing the elephant away.

The queen trusted that they had found a solution. "If you think this is the answer, then this is exactly what we will do. It's a brilliant idea, just brilliant," said the queen. She smiled as she walked away.

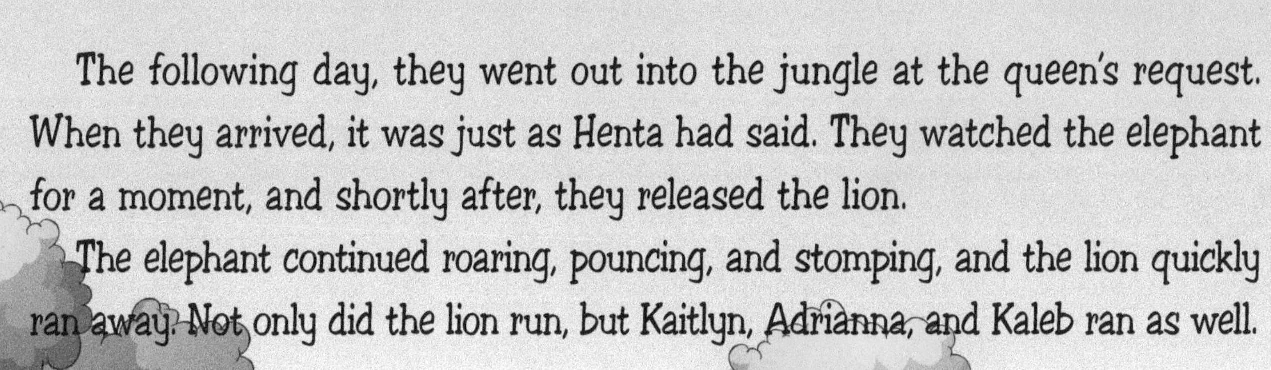

The following day, they went out into the jungle at the queen's request. When they arrived, it was just as Henta had said. They watched the elephant for a moment, and shortly after, they released the lion.

The elephant continued roaring, pouncing, and stomping, and the lion quickly ran away. Not only did the lion run, but Kaitlyn, Adrianna, and Kaleb ran as well.

They did not like the idea of returning to the queen's castle and telling her that their plan had failed. But they knew it had to be done, so off they went.

When they saw the queen, Kaitlyn quickly blurted out, "Good news, your highness; we found that we must make another plan and try again."

"Very well," said the queen. The group walked past the queen with smiles, but as soon as they were out of her sight, the sound of disappointment filled the room. Everyone took a deep breath and let out a loud sigh.

Henta flew in the room. She said, "You have been very brave. Don't worry; you will figure it out." And then she flew away.

They went back into the meeting room. Guards outside could hear low voices and papers rattling and smell the aroma of hot chocolate.

When the group had finished, they sent for the queen. Her heels could be heard clicking and clacking as she came down the long hallway. The large door opened and in walked the queen.

The advisors uncovered the new picture; this time it showed an angry bear chasing a frightened elephant. They showed the queen the new idea.

She said to them, "Very well, then. If you think this will work, then this is exactly what we will do. It's an interesting idea, very interesting," she said.

The following day, they went into the jungle at the queen's request. Shortly after they arrived, the bear was released. They all nervously watched to see what would happen. When the bear heard the elephant roaring, he turned and saw the elephant pouncing and stomping. Then he quickly ran away.

And of course, Adrianna, Kaitlyn, and Kaleb were not too far behind. It was another disappointing attempt. And once more they would have to tell the queen that their plan had failed.

When they saw the queen, Kaitlyn quickly blurted out, "Good news, your highness! We found that we must make a few more changes to our plan and try again."

"Very well," said the queen.

Then it was time for yet another meeting. This time, the meeting lasted longer than usual, and the advisors decided to do something a little different.

Again, they sent for the queen. Her heels could be heard clicking and clacking as she came down the long hallway. The large doors opened, and the queen appeared.

"Your highness," Adrianna said, "take a look at this." Kaitlyn uncovered the picture, and this time, it showed an angry skunk spraying a frightened elephant.

Kaitlyn said, "The elephant will not be able to stand the smell." Oh, how they hoped it would work this time.

Queen Autumn nodded and said, "Very well. If you think this will work, then this is exactly what we will do. It's a brilliant idea, just brilliant."

The following day, they arrived in the jungle at the queen's request. The elephant was still roaring, stomping, and pouncing. Keeping their fingers crossed, they released the skunk.

It did indeed spray the elephant. But instead of the elephant running, the skunk quickly ran away. And once again, Adrianna, Kaitlyn, and Kaleb were not far behind. It was another disappointing attempt. And once more they would have to tell the queen that their plan had failed.

Unfortunately, the solution had created yet another problem. The smell from the skunk was so bad that it slowed down their plans, and they decided not to return to the jungle for three days. During that time, the advisors made plan after plan after plan, but nothing seemed like it would work.

The table was covered with notes of ideas and Kaitlyn's drawings. Two days had passed, and they weren't any closer to a solution. The sad advisors had begun walking with their heads down and pacing back and forth. Kaitlyn felt so bad that they could not solve the problem for the queen.

On the third and final meeting day, the little bird Henta came with some very important news. Darting around, up, and down, she exclaimed, "Maya is passing through this town in two days!"

Maya was a seven-year-old orphan girl who lived with her grandparents. Although she was a child, she was well respected by many, and her fame had already reached the castle. She was known as the wisest kid in all the land.

The advisors were excited, and they sent a telegram to Maya asking whether she would be able to meet with the queen.

Maya responded, "It would be my great pleasure to meet with the queen."

When the queen found out, she was delighted and also relieved.

Maya had spent so many nights dreaming of meeting the queen. She would often leave her bed at night and sleep in the barn. She would dress up in her royal dress, which she had made out of some old curtains. And she would put a crown of straw on her head. The hay was her throne, and she would sit on it with pride.

On many nights, Maya stared at the stars through the window of the barn and dreamed she lived in a beautiful castle. The wind lifted her hair so gently, and it fell upon her back, swinging from side to side. She shivered as she felt the chill exit her body. Then she sang the most beautiful songs to the stars. Her grandparents could hear her singing in the barn. When she stopped singing, they knew she was asleep, and they went to the barn and covered her with a blanket.

The next morning, her grandparents asked her how she slept, even though they knew she had not slept in her bed. And she replied, "I had the most beautiful dream!"

But this was no ordinary dream. No, not at all. "This was a special dream," she said as she gazed into the distance. "It's the kind of dream that you dream when you are awake and your eyes are wide open. And there is no distance and no time."

As she stood there smiling, she forgot she still had the straw crown on her head.

When Maya arrived in Jungle Land, Queen Autumn invited her into the castle and offered her food and drinks. They all had quite a party. Later that day, it was time for a meeting to see what could be done about the angry elephant. The sketch artist, planners, and interpreters were all in place.

They quickly brought Maya into the meeting room and wanted to sketch out her ideas. But Maya insisted on not making any plans. She said, "I must see for myself what is going on with the elephant. After all, how can I solve a problem when I don't even know what the problem is yet?"

The room became very quiet as everyone marveled at the wisdom of the little girl. They wondered why they had not thought of it themselves.

The next morning, after they ate breakfast, off to the jungle they went. The elephant appeared increasingly angry. Maya walked around the entire area and looked at everything except the elephant. Everyone was confused as they watched her.

But Henta knew exactly what she was doing. After a few minutes, she said, "Okay, please take me back to the castle."

And off they went. They wondered what she had discovered, but they did not dare to ask.

The queen was happy to see Maya. "Maya, my dear, have you found a solution to our problem in the animal kingdom?"

"Yes, Your Highness, I have found the answer. And I know just what to do."

"Very well, then," replied the queen. "I will see to it that you have everything you need." Then she called together the advisors and told them to give Maya everything she needed, including any animal.

Maya turned to them and asked, "Do you have some cheese?"

"Cheese? You want a snack right now?" asked Kaitlyn.

"No, I don't want a snack. I need cheese, wire, string, and wood."

They laughed at how cute it sounded. Then Queen Autumn looked seriously at the staff and said, "You heard the child! Gather the supplies!"

The laughter quickly stopped. Silence filled the air.

Then Maya said, "I will also need some beautiful fabric."

"And what will you do with that beautiful fabric?" asked Kaleb.

"I will use the fabric to ride back on the nice elephant," said Maya.

"Ride back on the nice elephant?" Kaitlyn asked as she laughed.

"Nice elephant? But the elephant is dangerous," said Adrianna.

The queen gave them a stern look.

Maya taught them how to make traps. They did as they were told, but they could not figure out how they were going to catch the big elephant in the little traps.

Off they went to the jungle. In the bushes a family of mice had made a nest with their babies. Maya knew that instead of being an angry elephant, it was actually a very scared elephant.

Maya whispered to Henta, "Fly down quietly and fast to lock the cage once all the mice are inside."

By sundown they had captured all the mice. Kaitlyn, Adrianna, and Kaleb sat and waited for the big elephant to get inside the small cage. They did not understand because the elephant was nowhere near the cage.

Then Maya said, "Okay, let's load up."

Everyone was confused because the elephant was still there.

"Not for long," Maya said.

So they gathered the traps with the mice in them and took them away.

The elephant immediately stopped stomping and bouncing and began walking calmly again. The advisors prepared to take the good news back to the queen.

Maya placed the beautiful fabric on the elephant and rode back into town on the elephant's back, just as she had planned. She placed her straw crown on her head, and Henta sat on her shoulder.

When the queen saw her, she was very impressed. Was this the elephant that had been so angry? In fact, she was so impressed that she offered Maya her own room in the castle.

Maya thanked her but said, "I must go home to my grandparents because they are my only family."

The queen said, "I have an idea! What if we move your grandparents into the castle too?"

Maya stared in disbelief. "Okay, sure!" she replied.

Maya's grandparents agreed to move into the castle. As always, Maya stood in the window and sang her songs to the stars. She still put her crown of straw on her head. She didn't have to dream anymore, though; she was living her dream in the castle.

The queen tried to give her a beautiful crown. But Maya whispered, "Put it on my grandmother's head instead since I love the straw crown that I made."

Meanwhile, the elephant's fame had reached many, and everyone wanted to see it. Kaitlyn, Kaleb, and Adrianna taught the elephant many tricks.

The mice had become very good at juggling cheese balls and walking on tiny ropes.

And most important of all, the elephant and the mice were no longer afraid of each other. They often did tricks together for their eager fans. Henta loved her new animal friends.

Soon a circus was born. It would be an amazing addition to Happy Day-Circus Day! And once again there was peace in the animal kingdom and excitement in Jungle Land. Moreover, it would not be the last time the queen had to call on Maya to save the day.

The End

Moral of the Story:

You have to understand the cause of the problem before you can solve the problem. And little kids are wiser than we think.

# About the Author

**Safiya Wilcox** has been writing since she was in fourth grade. She loves using her imagination to create stories with morals for her children. This is her first book.

CPSIA information can be obtained
at www.ICGtesting.com
Printed in the USA
LVHW070052121220
673999LV00023B/440

9 781480 896109